How to be a hero

This book is not like others you may have read. You are the hero of this adventure. It is up to you to make decisions that will affect how the adventure unfolds.

Each section of this book is numbered. At the end of most sections, you will have to make a choice. The choice you make will take you to a different section of the book.

Some of your choices will help you to complete the adventure successfully. But choose carefully, some of your decisions could be fatal!

If you fail, then start the adventure again and learn from your mistake.

If you choose correctly you will succeed in your mission.

Don't be a zero, be a hero!

You are a member of a Special Forces military unit. You have taken part in dangerous missions and have won medals for your bravery.

You have also flown many secret military planes, and even tested prototype space vehicles and advanced weapons. You are the top-ranking test pilot in the force.

After your latest Special Forces mission, you are taking some well-earned rest. You are relaxing at home, watching a news bulletin. There are reports of strange weather patterns across the world. Typhoons, hurricanes, thunderstorms and sandstorms are battering cities, causing death and destruction across the planet.

At that moment your doorbell rings. You open the door to reveal a man and a woman, both dressed in stiff black suits. They show you their IDs.

"Agent Roberts," the man says, "and this is Agent Lee. We're with Earth Defence."

"Never heard of it," you say.

"That's because it's a top-secret unit," replies Roberts.

"We need your help," says Lee.

TYRANNO QUEST

AIR BLAST

eve Barlow and Steve Skidmore
Illustrated by Jack Lawrence

First published in 2012
by Franklin Watts

Text © Steve Barlow and Steve Skidmore 2012
Illustrations by Jack Lawrence © Franklin Watts 2012
Cover design by Jonathan Hair
The "2Steves" illustrations by Paul Davidson
used by kind permission of Orchard Books

Franklin Watts
338 Euston Road
London NW1 3BH

Franklin Watts Australia
Level 17/207 Kent Street
Sydney, NSW 2000

A CIP catalogue record for this book
is available from the British Library.

ISBN: 978 1 4451 0875 9

"Well, OK then. You'd better come in," you say. They follow you inside.

"Have you seen the reports of severe weather?" asks Agent Lee.

You nod. "Is global warming causing it?"

Roberts shakes his head. "No, it's more than that. Earth is being attacked."

"Attacked by what?" you ask.

Agent Lee shakes her head. "We'll brief you when we get to Area 61."

You look puzzled. "Don't you mean Area 51, the top-secret US military base in the Nevada desert? I've never heard of Area 61."

She nods. "Exactly — it's above top secret!" You smile. "Ultra secret? Sounds interesting. Let's get going..."

Go to section 1.

1

Roberts and Lee escort you to a nearby military base, where a helicopter is waiting. Soon all three of you are flying across country to Area 61. The weather becomes worse. Rain starts to hammer down on the helicopter windscreen. Lightning flashes across the sky.

"This is bad," shouts the pilot. "Maybe we should land."

Before you can reply, a bolt of lightning strikes the helicopter. It lurches sideways and the pilot's head smashes against the cockpit window. He is knocked out and slumps against the joystick.

The helicopter begins to spin out of control. You have to react quickly or you will all die!

To try to wake up the pilot, go to 14.

To try to fly the helicopter, go to 37.

2

"Full attack," you order.

Your suit responds and streams of energy head towards Hurrikano. But before they can hit him, his Staff of Power forms a defensive shield. The bolts ricochet around the room.

With a flick of the staff, Hurrikano flies across the room and attacks you with lightning bolts. You dodge the missiles and return fire with your needle gun. Again, his defensive shield renders your attack harmless.

If you want to try to distract Hurrikano by talking to him, go to 43.

If you wish to continue the fight, go to 21.

3

You start to make your way across the cloud, keeping a careful eye on the winged forces.

Suddenly, two robot drones appear and hover before you. They emit strange noises and your DART suit translates.

"Who are you and what are you doing?"

If you wish to talk to the drones, go to 30.
If you wish to fight your way out, go to 22.

4

"It sounds dangerous and right up my street," you say. "But how do I get to this Airworld?"

"You use one of my inventions," says QTee. He presses a button and a wall opens up to reveal an amazing-looking robotic suit.

"This is a Defence and Armed-Response Teleportation suit, or DART for short. It allows the wearer to teleport between planets and dimensions. It protects him or her from enemies and hostile environments. And it carries a number of weapons."

You are impressed. "What sort of firepower does it have?" you ask.

"It has a variety of weapons systems and you can even control these by speaking or just by thinking!"

"We don't have much time, so you'd better start learning about the suit," says Agent Lee.

Go to 34.

5

"Arm and fire TD bomb," you order.

The bomb shoots into the body of the gas giant and explodes. But to your horror, the creature isn't killed. Instead, it absorbs the energy of the bomb and grows bigger!

Before you can react, the creature fires dozens of huge gas bombs at you. They explode, creating an intense heat. The DART's circuits burn. You cannot defend yourself. You glance up to see the giant standing above you. It sends another stream of bombs your way. You are blasted into oblivion.

Begin your mission again by going to 1.

6

Two blasts of energy from your eGun finish off the creature.

You look around, still wondering how you are going to get to the upper cloud belt. The airfield is still a hive of activity.

If you want to teleport back to Earth, go to 41.

If you want to head to the airfield, go to 3.

7

"We've got to land," you shout. "Flying in this weather will kill us."

You push down on the joystick and manage to bring the helicopter safely to the ground.

You breathe a sigh of relief. "Sometimes you have to know when it's just too dangerous to battle against the elements."

"Funny you should say that," says Agent Lee. "But this is nothing, compared to what is coming your way. I wonder if you're up for it?"

If you want to go back home, go to 49.

If you want to find out about the mission, go to 42.

8

"Speed mode," you order. The DART suit responds and you head away from the creatures. One of them follows you, sucking at the air with incredible force.

Suddenly you spin around and run past the creature towards the other storm reaper. The first creature turns and heads after you. You are now heading straight into the mouth of one of the reapers, whilst the other one is right behind you.

Just as it seems as though you are going to be sucked into the creature's mouth, you shout, "Super speed!" and turn to your right. The suit responds and you just avoid the storm reaper's deadly blades.

However, the other storm reaper isn't so lucky. The creatures smash into each other. Their rotating blades tear at their bodies. There is a sound of squealing and roaring, and then silence as the creatures disappear in the blink of an eye.

You breathe a sigh of relief and head towards Hurrikano's palace.

Go to 24.

9

As you raise your hands in surrender, you hear a shot. An energy bolt hits you. The pain is excruciating and you pass out.

When you wake up, you find yourself in a prison cell. Your DART suit has been removed.

You shout out, but no one answers. You

realise that you will die on Airworld, and Earth will be destroyed.

Mission failed! Go back to 1.

10

You stare wide-eyed at the alien creature.

"This is QTee — he's Earth Defence's technical genius," explains Agent Roberts. "Earth Defence is an ultra top-secret unit. Our task is to stop alien races attacking Earth."

"But he's an alien," you point out.

"There are good aliens and bad aliens. He's one of the good ones."

QTee smiles and nods at the gun. "And this beauty is a new toy I'm working on. It cancels out the effects of gravity." He stares at you. "And you are the one who is volunteering for this mission in which you are almost certain to die. Are you up to it?"

To find out more about the mission, go to 23.

If you decide you don't want any part of this adventure, go to 49.

You fire a volley of energy bolts and missiles at the window shutters.

A gaping hole appears and the effects of the bomb are cancelled. However, the control room is destroyed and the palace begins to drop down through the sky.

You open the DART's power unit and slip Hurrikano's crystal inside. Let's hope QTee was right, you think as you leap through the hole. You start to drop. Around you hundreds of winged creatures are pouring from out of the doomed palace.

Fly, you think. Incredibly the suit responds to your thoughts. The crystal does work! You fly away from the palace towards the lower cloud levels. You land and order the DART suit to teleport you back to Earth.

Go to 50.

"Navigate the route to the palace," you order.

"Head to the upper cloud belt," replies the DART's NAV system.

You look up and see more clouds. They also have buildings on them. Many creatures are flying between the cloud belts, but they all have wings. You wonder how you are going to get to the upper clouds.

As you stare skywards, a huge creature circles above you. It is a cross between a huge bird of prey and a dark cloud. It squawks at you, spitting a lightning bolt from its beak. The bolt just misses you.

"DANGER! Cyclone hawk!" cries the DART suit's computer as the hawk dives at you with its deadly steel talons outstretched.

If you want to kill the hawk, go to 35.

If you want to try and capture it, go to 44.

If you want to teleport back to Earth, go to 41.

As you walk by the objects, you hear a humming noise, which turns into a deafening roar.

"DANGER! DANGER!" warns the DART suit.

Before you can react there is a huge rush of wind. The objects transform into enormous tunnels of spinning black clouds reaching up into the sky.

Their mouths open from within the depths of the black cloud, to reveal sets of rotating blades! Like a hurricane, the wind sucks you towards the gaping mouth of one of the creatures.

"STORM REAPERS!"

You can hardly hear yourself think as you are pulled towards the maelstrom and the rotating blades.

If you want to teleport back to Earth, go to 41.

If you want to try to blow up the creatures with a bomb, go to 38.

If you want to use your eGun, go to 29.

14

As the helicopter spins wildly through the air, you reach over and shake the pilot. It is hopeless; the man is unconscious.

"Take over the controls," yells Agent Lee.

You push the pilot out of the way, and wrestle with the joystick. Just as you think you have things under control, another gust of wind blasts the helicopter.

Go to 26.

15

You fire a stream of eGun energy bolts into the body of the gas giant.

To your amazement, the creature absorbs the energy and fires them back at you!

You just avoid being killed by your own shots!

The creature points its finger and unleashes a volley of flaming gas bombs, which explode around you.

To continue the fight, go to 27.

To teleport back to Earth, go to 41.

If you wish to take advice from the DART computer, go to 46.

16

You put the eGun to the creature's head. "You will take me to the upper cloud belt or die," you say. The DART suit translates. The creature squawks and nods its head.

Carefully, you release some of the bonds that are holding the hawk captive. You climb onto its back and clamp the suit to the hawk's body. "Let's fly!"

The creature takes off and within seconds you arrive at the upper cloud belt. You order the hawk to land out of view of Hurrikano's forces. The creature obeys.

As you climb down, the creature tears at the net with its talons. The steel ropes give way and it takes to the air.

If you want to kill the cyclone hawk, go to 33.

If you want to let it escape, go to 25.

17

"Tell me more about the bombs," you say.

"The TD bomb is a total destruction bomb," replies QTee. "It is like a mini atom bomb. It can destroy all solid objects within a diameter of a hundred metres. The molecular bomb changes the molecular structure of an enemy. For instance, an enemy could be melted or turned into a gas."

If you want to choose the TD bomb, go to 28.
To choose the molecular bomb, go to 39.

18

"Stealth and speed mode," you tell the suit. Your enemies do not see you as you hurry across the bridge. You deal quickly with a winged guard standing at the entrance of the palace, using your eGun to silence him.

As you enter the palace, the door slams shut behind you. There is a noise of engines and the floor judders. The flying palace is on the move!

"Search for Hurrikano," you order.

Within seconds, the computer has a fix on your target. You begin to follow the route on your NAV system, but as you turn a corner, you meet a patrol of flying robot drones.

A drone speaks. "Intruder! Surrender!"

If you wish to surrender, go to 9.
If you want to attack the drones, go to 36.

"Scan objects," you order.

Seconds later the computer replies. "DANGER! Objects are storm reapers. Weapons are useless against them."

At that moment there is a humming noise, which turns into a deafening roar. The objects transform into enormous tunnels of spinning black clouds, reaching into the sky.

Their mouths open from within the depths of the black cloud to reveal sets of rotating blades! Like a hurricane, the wind sucks you towards the gaping mouth of one of the creatures. You can hardly hear yourself think as you are pulled towards the maelstrom and the rotating blades.

To teleport back to Earth, go to 41.
To try to blow up the creatures with a bomb, go to 38.
If you want to use your eGun, go to 29.
To try and trick the creatures, go to 8.

20

"What are you doing, you crazy fool!" you cry and reach over to the controls.

"No!" shouts the pilot. The agents scream at you to stop, but you ignore them. You wrestle with the pilot for the controls. In the struggle, you manage to grab the joystick, but the helicopter lurches down towards the forest.

The pilot realises that you are doomed and scrabbles at the emergency door release, leaving you to fly the helicopter.

Go to 26.

Your attacks with energy bolts and lasers are useless against Hurrikano's Staff of Power. You have only one more weapon left to try.

"Arm vacuum bomb." You aim at the control room floor. "Fire."

The bomb launches, hits the ground and explodes.

Hurrikano laughs. "A poor shot!"

"I don't think so." The walls suddenly shudder. There is a roaring noise as the air is sucked from the room.

"You sealed the room and this is a vacuum bomb. Take away the air and there is nothing for you to control," you explain. You point your eGun at him.

Hurrikano holds out his staff, but it is powerless. A laser blast hits him in the chest and he falls to the ground. The staff clatters onto the floor. You pick it up, snap it in half and remove the power crystal.

Hurrikano looks up at you. "You think that I am the only one to threaten your miserable little planet. There are more on their way. My master, Tyranno, will destroy the Earth." They are Hurrikano's last words.

At that moment there is a terrible grinding noise. The room is collapsing in on itself as the bomb continues its work.

If you want to teleport back to Earth, go to 32.

If you wish to try to blast your way out of the room, go to 11.

22

Before the drones can ask any more questions, you blast them with your eGun. Bolts of pure energy zap into their metal shells and they explode.

However, your attack attracts the attention of other creatures. You are outnumbered as dozens of armed drones and winged beings surround you.

If you want to surrender, go to 9.

If you wish to fight, go to 48.

If you wish to teleport back to Earth, go to 41.

23

"Of course I am," you reply. "Tell me more."

"Follow us." The agents and QTee take you through corridors, deep into the mountain side. Finally you arrive at a set of doors marked OPS ROOM. The doors open and you walk in.

You sit at a desk and Agent Roberts begins to explain. "Earth has been attacked many times before by different alien races. Earth Defence is here to defend it against such attacks.

"We believe that these strange weather patterns are the latest attack. Our INTEL people have been monitoring intergalactic communications, and this is what we've come up with."

He slides a tablet to you across the desk. You begin to read.

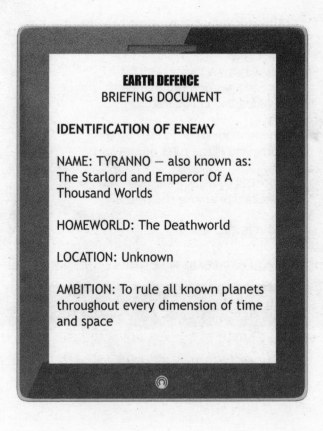

EARTH DEFENCE
BRIEFING DOCUMENT

IDENTIFICATION OF ENEMY

NAME: TYRANNO — also known as: The Starlord and Emperor Of A Thousand Worlds

HOMEWORLD: The Deathworld

LOCATION: Unknown

AMBITION: To rule all known planets throughout every dimension of time and space

BACKGROUND INFORMATION

Tyranno has placed his followers to rule planets throughout the galaxies and dimensions.

These governors have each been given a Staff of Power that they use to enforce their rule.

Tyranno has ordered that Earth is to be invaded and conquered.

The first governor to take up this command is the ruler of Airworld.

AIRWORLD: A gas giant planet whose people live among the clouds

GOVERNOR: Hurrikano

LOCATION: Nexus dimension

Agent Lee speaks up. "Hurrikano is using his Staff of Power to open up the dimensions and control the elements of air, here on Earth. When he has caused enough destruction, his forces will invade."

"So why am I here?" you ask.

Agent Lee stares at you. "We need you to go to Airworld, defeat Hurrikano and save Earth from total destruction. It's a highly dangerous mission."

If you want to undertake the mission, go to 4.

If you don't want to risk your life, go to 49.

24

You finally arrive at Hurrikano's palace. It is not resting on a cloud; it is floating in the sky. You realise that it is a huge flying machine.

There is a long, narrow cloud bridge leading to the palace. The way is guarded by a huge figure that shimmers and moves in the wind. The tips of its fingers burn with fire and black smoke belches out from its mouth.

"DANGER! Gas giant," warns the DART's computer.

If you wish to attack the giant immediately, go to 15.

If you wish to take advice from the DART suit computer, go to 46.

25

As the hawk flies off, you hear it squawking as if raising an alarm. Sure enough, seconds later, the air is filled with winged beings of all shapes and sizes. They are heading your way!

The air is filled with laser streams, lightning bolts and mini-tornado bombs as they attack you in waves.

You return fire, but your DART suit takes several hits.

If you wish to teleport back to Earth, go to 41.

If you prefer to keep on fighting, go to 48.

26

You do your best to try to keep the helicopter flying, but the engine stalls, causing the rotor blades to stop turning. The helicopter plummets downwards. Frantically, you try to restart the engine, but time runs out. The helicopter smashes into the ground and explodes in a fireball.

Ouch! Try harder and go back to 1.

27

You change weapons to your needle laser and fire at the gas giant. You launch missiles, too.

Once again, the laser streams and missiles are absorbed and shot back at you. You try to avoid them, but one of the deadly light beams hits you. The computer doesn't respond to any of your commands.

"Teleport!" you scream, but it is hopeless. The gas giant fires a stream of gas bombs.

You try to move, but cannot. There is an explosion of light, and then only silence...

You have paid the ultimate price. Begin again and go to 1.

"I'll take the TD bomb," you tell QTee.

"Okie doke." He loads the bomb into the DART suit launcher. "Now it's time for you to teleport to Airworld. Remember you can only use teleportation to and from Earth, not to move around Airworld."

You enter the suit and it locks into place around you. You hear QTee talking to you over the COMS link.

"I have set the teleportation co-ordinates to Airworld. I can't get you near Hurrikano's palace as there is some sort of teleport block on it. You will have to make your own way there, and once inside you won't be able to teleport out, so be careful! I have also set the NAV system to guide you. Use it! Once you have defeated Hurrikano, and are in teleportation range, get back to Earth. Good luck!"

I'm going to need it, you think.

"Teleport begin."

There is a bright white light and you feel as though your body is being ripped into a million pieces.

Go to 47.

29

You fire repeatedly at the storm reapers, until your eGun overheats. But the creatures merely absorb the energy.

You are being dragged closer and closer towards the creatures' deadly mouths.

To teleport back to Earth, go to 41.

If you want to try to blow up the creatures with a bomb, go to 38.

30

"I have arrived from planet Earth," you reply. "I have been spying for Hurrikano. I have important news."

The drones are silent. They are obviously checking this information.

Finally, one of the drones speaks, "There is no record of such a spy."

"Because the mission was secret!" you say.

"There is no record of such a spy," repeats the drone, and a laser gun emerges from its metal body.

To attack the drones, go to 22.

To teleport back to Earth, go to 41.

"Are you sure you know what you're doing?"
you ask.

"Trust me," smiles the pilot. Just as it seems
as though you are going to crash, the side of
the mountain opens up and you fly in.

"Do you like our secret entrance?" says the
pilot, as two huge steel doors close behind you.
He lands the helicopter in a large hangar.

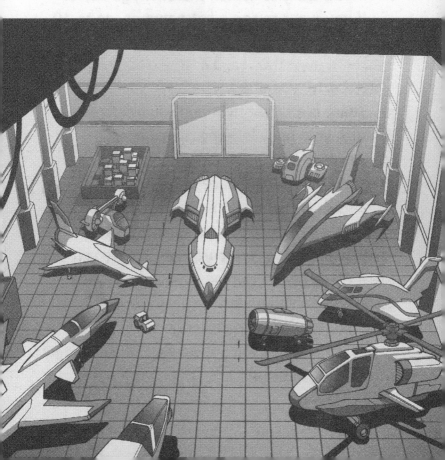

"Impressive," you reply.

"Welcome to Area 61," says Agent Roberts. "This is the HQ of Earth Defence. It's time to find out what you've let yourself in for!"

You head across the hangar to a set of doors. They swish open and you give a cry of alarm. Standing straight ahead of you is an alien creature, pointing a huge gun at you!

If you want to attack the alien, go to 45.
If you want to see what happens, go to 10.

32

"Teleport," you order.

There is a bright light and you briefly feel as though your body is being ripped apart.

You open your eyes and gasp in horror. You are still inside the palace's control room! The room is rapidly falling in on itself. You remember what QTee said about the palace being blocked for teleportation. Before you can react, you hear a ripping noise — your DART suit has cracked under the pressure of the vacuum! You have no protection. Your bones begin to crack as you are slowly and agonisingly crushed to death.

You defeated Hurrikano, but it has cost you your life.

Begin your adventure again by going to 1.

33

You know that you cannot let the creature raise the alarm.

A flash shoots from your needle laser and hits the hawk. It drops from the sky.

"Head north," orders the NAV system. "Stealth mode."

You make your way across the clouds, being careful to avoid Hurrikano's creatures. Sometime later you see in the distance, a huge metal building.

"Hurrikano's palace ahead," says the NAV system.

You make your way towards it, passing through fields of clouds. You look ahead and see two strange, egg-shaped objects, nestling on the ground.

If you want to investigate these, go to 19.

If you wish to carry on to the palace, go to 13.

Roberts and Lee leave you with QTee, and over the next few hours you learn about the suit and how to use it. The DART suit has a number of weapons systems.

QTee also tells you about how to gain extra powers for the suit. "We think that if you capture Hurrikano's staff, take the crystal that powers it and install it in your suit's power unit, you will be able to use it to control the element of air. Your suit will be able to fly!"

He also arms the suit with a vacuum bomb, which will suck out all the air in a confined space. "It will counter Hurrikano's power over the air, easy peasy. If there's no air, he'll have no power," says QTee. "You also have a choice of one more bomb. You can take a TD bomb or a molecular bomb."

If you want to know more about the weapons, go to 17.

If you want to choose the TD bomb, go to 28.

If you want to choose the molecular bomb, go to 39.

DART suit weapons systems

↑ eGun – main arm-mounted, medium-power weapon, fires energy bolts

↑ Needle laser – arm-mounted, light-power weapon, rapid fire

↑ Missile launcher – shoulder-mounted, fires explosive missiles and also QTee's special bombs

→ Net launcher – arm-mounted, fires steel web net to catch and snare

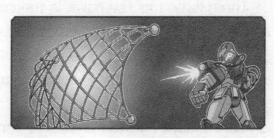

↓ Speed function – run twice as fast over a short distance. Also has "super speed" for x4 speed burst.

↓ NAV system – a guidance system to help you find your way. QTee says, "Use it!"

→ Power unit – storage cell for crystals that you find. New crystals give the DART suit new powers.

Other special features:
Poly-absorption armour

Teleportation unit

Stealth mode — you can sneak past enemies

The hawk flies at you, spinning and turning at an incredible speed.

You prime your weapons system to attack mode.

"Missile launcher ready," says the computer.

"Fire!" you order.

The missile hits the hawk in its chest and explodes. The creature is knocked backwards, but only for a moment. It continues its attack. Another bolt of lightning shoots from its beak.

"Continuous firing!" you order.

More missiles hit the creature. The assault is successful. The cyclone hawk drops dazed, at your feet. You shoot a steel net around the creature to make sure it cannot attack further.

If you wish to kill the creature, go to 6.

If you think you can use the hawk to help you, go to 16.

"Full attack," you order and blast at the drones with your needle laser and eGun. The drones are no match for your firepower, and they are blasted to pieces.

You speed down corridors towards Hurrikano's control room, dealing quickly with any enemies that have the misfortune to get in your way.

"Target ahead," warns the NAV system.

You open a metal door and step through it into a control room. The door shuts behind you and window shutters slam down, blocking out all outside light.

You hear a rustle and a figure lands on the floor before you. You have found your enemy!

"So, you have finally arrived," says Hurrikano. "I've been following your progress with interest. But now you are trapped. This control room is sealed off. There is no escape."

If you wish to attack Hurrikano, go to 2.
If you wish to talk to him, go to 43.

37

You push the pilot out of the way and grab hold of the controls. The helicopter is spinning wildly. Using all your strength and skill you pull on the joystick and manage to bring the helicopter under control.

"They said you were a top pilot," says Agent Roberts.

"Tell me that when we're safe," you reply. "We're not out of the storm yet!"

If you want to land the helicopter, go to 7.

If you want to fly through the storm, go to 26.

38

"Arm bomb and fire!" you shout.

The bomb launches into the mouth of one of the storm reapers. It hits the rotating blades — but nothing happens!

You are in a state of shock. Before you can rearm your weapons system, the storm reaper sucks you into its deadly mouth. You hit the blades and feel nothing more.

Try to stay alive next time! Go to 1.

"I'll take the molecular bomb," you tell QTee.

"Okie doke." He fits the bomb into the DART suit launcher. "Now it's time for you to teleport to Airworld. Remember you can only use teleportation to and from Earth, not to move around Airworld."

You enter the suit and it closes around you. You hear QTee talking to you over the COMS link.

"I have worked out the teleportation co-ordinates to Airworld. I can't get you near Hurrikano's palace as there is some sort of teleport block on it. You will have to make your own way there, and once inside you won't be able to teleport out, so be careful! I have set the NAV system, to guide you. Use it! Once you have defeated Hurrikano and are in teleportation range, get back to Earth. Good luck!"

I'm going to need it, you think.

"Teleport begin."

There is a bright white light and you feel as though your body is being ripped into a million pieces.

Go to 47.

40

"Arm and fire molecular bomb," you order.

The bomb hurtles into the body of the gas giant and explodes. For a few seconds it looks as though the bomb hasn't worked, and the giant strides towards you, ready to attack. You hear a series of explosions and jets of flame shoot from out of the creature's body. The gas giant's molecular structure begins to change! The fires set off a chain reaction and the creature's body collapses in on itself and falls to the ground.

"Enemy compromised," says the DART's computer.

You arm your eGun and send volley after volley of energy bolts into the creature's body.

A huge fireball fills the sky as the giant explodes. Alarms begin to sound from the palace, and dozens of attack drones and armed winged beings fly out to investigate.

If you wish to attack them, go to 48.
If you wish to head to the palace, go to 18.

41

"Teleport," you order your DART suit.

There is a bright light and you find yourself back in the OPS room.

QTee looks at you in surprise. "Why have you abandoned the mission?"

"It was getting a little tricky," you reply. "I needed to get out, but don't worry, I'll go back again."

QTee shakes his head. "You can go home. You are not up to this task. We will find someone who is more heroic than you."

If you are feeling more heroic and wish to begin again, go back to 1.

42

"Of course I am," you say. "Bring it on!"

Within half an hour the helicopter pilot has recovered, the weather has calmed down and you are back in the air.

Sometime later you are flying over a vast pine forest, heading directly towards the side of a mountain. The pilot increases speed! You wonder if the pilot's bang on the head is affecting his ability to fly.

The mountain side gets closer and closer!

To take control of the helicopter, go to 20.
If you trust the pilot, go to 31.

43

"What do you intend to do?" you ask.

"Eliminate you," he replies. Before you can react, a lightning bolt flashes from his Staff of Power. It hits you in the chest. Another lightning bolt rips your suit open.

"I don't have time to explain myself to such a creature as you. I have a world to destroy."

The last thing you see is a flash of lightning.

You are dead. Begin again by going to 1.

44

The hawk flies at you, spinning and turning at an incredible speed. It spits bolts of lightning at you.

You prime your weapons system into a defend-and-capture mode. The suit takes several hits, but its armour is too strong to be damaged.

"Launch net," you order.

A steel net shoots from your arm launcher. It hits the cyclone hawk and snares it. The creature drops to the ground, wrapped up like a trussed-up chicken.

If you wish to kill the creature, go to 6.

If you think you can use the hawk to help you, go to 16.

45

You leap towards the alien, but before you can hit it, the creature fires. A blue bolt hits you and you find yourself floating above the ground, powerless to move your arms and legs!

"This is our hero?" says the alien. "He's a bit of a lightweight!"

The agents laugh. "Let him down, QTee," orders Agent Lee.

"Okie doke. I wouldn't want to keep him hanging around," replies QTee. The alien switches off the gun and you drop to the floor, unhurt, except for your pride.

Go to 10.

46

"What is the attack strategy?" you ask.

"Gas giants absorb all energy and laser weaponry," replies the computer. "Bomb attack is recommended."

If you chose the TD bomb, go to 5.
If you chose the molecular bomb, go to 40.

47

The white light dies away and the pain subsides. You look around. You are standing on a huge cloud. All around there are buildings floating on clouds! You have made it to Airworld.

Some way ahead of you is a huge airfield. Incredible flying machines are landing and taking off. Hundreds of winged alien beings fly around, carrying weapons and supplies. You realise that these must be Hurrikano's forces, getting ready to invade Earth.

If you want to head to the airfield, go to 3.
If you wish to use your NAV system, go to 12.

48

You begin shooting, but there are too many enemies to deal with. You are hit time after time with energy bolts and laser beams.

Your DART suit is unable to stand up to the firepower and you slump to the ground. Your weapons system is destroyed. You have no defence against the final stream of energy bolts that send you into oblivion.

You can begin your adventure again, just go to 1.

49

You shake your head. "This is too much for me. I don't want to risk my life in some crazy scheme," you say. "Take me home."

Agent Roberts nods. "So you're not the hero everyone thinks you are. Glad we found out now, rather than when it mattered."

You head for home, not knowing what could have been.

When you feel brave enough to begin the mission again, go to 1.

There is a flash of light and you find yourself back in the OPS room in Area 61.

QTee is waiting for you.

"Welcome back," he says. "You'll be glad to know that the weather is back to normal. It looks like you succeeded!"

You open the DART suit's power unit and show him the crystal.

"I'll hardwire this into the suit permanently. From now on, you'll be able to use the DART suit to fly!"

"I think I'll be needing it soon," you reply. You tell him about Hurrikano's threat.

QTee looks grim. "We've won the battle, but not the war. I wonder what Tyranno is going to throw at us next?"

You succeeded! You are a hero!
Thanks to you, Earth is safe...
...for the time being...

About the 2Steves

"The 2Steves" are
Britain's most popular
writing double act
for young people,
specialising in comedy
and adventure. They

Steve Barlow and Steve Skidmore

perform regularly in schools and libraries,
and at festivals, taking the power of words
and story to audiences of all ages.

Together they have written many books,
including the *Crime Team* and *iHorror* series.

About the illustrator: Jack Lawrence

Jack Lawrence is a successful freelance
comics illustrator, working on titles such as
A.T.O.M., Cartoon Network, *Doctor Who
Adventures*, *2000 AD*, *Gogos Mega Metropolis*
and *Spider-Man Tower of Power*. He also works
as a freelance toy designer.

Lawrence lives in Maidstone in Kent with
his partner and two cats.

Creating I HERO Tyranno Quest...

We started wring the original I HERO for Franklin Watts/EDGE back in 2007. You could become the hero, such as a gladiator or a spy or an astronaut, and decide what happens in the adventure. With I HERO Quests we wanted to make the baddies even better, and to make the adventures longer over four different books.

We love thinking up different aliens. Tyranno is a really nasty piece of work, intent on taking over Earth, but his three lords — Hurrikano, Vulkana and Arktos — are pretty tough, too. And we know our readers will love beating them all to become the hero!

We even have a special I HERO roadshow which we run in schools and at festivals all over the world. That's the great thing about these books, they really bring the adventure to life!

So we really hope you like I HERO. Let us know what you think - we're on Twitter @the2Steves, or you can contact us via our website **www.the2steves.net**

I HERO
DECIDE YOUR OWN DESTINY
EDGE
TYRANNO QUEST
FIRE STORM
Steve Barlow - Steve Skidmore

TYRANNO QUEST
FIRE STORM

Steve Barlow and Steve Skidmore
Illustrated by Jack Lawrence

Tyranno, the evil Starlord, plans to attack Earth
with his alien armies. Your quest is to defeat
Tyranno. But before YOU can challenge him, you
must battle Vulkana, ruler of Fireworld. Defeat
Vulkana and capture her Staff of Power. Use it to
upgrade your DART suit with a brand-new ability!

You are the hero of this book.
Only you can decide your own destiny...

**Turn over to read the first
section of Fire Storm – and
to discover some of the
aliens you'll have
to battle...**

1

You are relaxing inside Area 61, talking to
Agents Roberts and Lee, when a voice breaks
over the COMs system. It is QTee. "Please come
to the OPS room. We have a situation."

"Looks like you've got another mission," says
Agent Lee.

You all hurry over to the OPS room.

QTee points at a large display screen.
"These volcanoes have all just erupted at the
same time!"

"Are we under attack again?" you ask.

QTee nods. "Another of Tyranno's followers has taken up from where Hurrikano left off. Our INTEL has told us that the attack is being led by Vulkana. She rules the planet of Fireworld, in the Altus dimension. Her Staff of Power gives her control over the element of fire. She has used it to activate hundreds of volcanoes that exist on Earth. We've got reports of clouds of ash and lava streams causing devastation and destruction across the planet."

Continue the adventure in
I HERO Tyranno Quest 2:

FIRE STORM

Discover some of the aliens from FIRE STORM...

Flame trolls — huge aliens who live on Fireworld. They have flame-throwers for weapons.

Fire titan — even more massive than a flame troll, these aliens have flame-thrower arms!

Pyrodogs —
these beasts guard
underground areas of
Vulkana's kingdom.
Oh, and they spit fire!

Fire imps —
they might look small, but they are armed with
flaming tar-ball slingshots — and there's lots of them!

Want to read more "You Are The Hero" adventures? Well, why not try these...

Also by the 2Steves: iHorror
Fight your fear. Choose your fate.

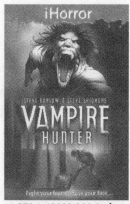

978 1 40830 985 8 pb
978 1 40831 476 0 eBook

978 1 40830 986 5 pb
978 1 40831 477 7 eBook

978 1 40830 988 9 pb
978 1 40831 479 1 eBook

978 1 40830 987 2 pb
978 1 40831 478 4 eBook